Winter F[...]

DRESSING FOR THE COLD

By Jasper Bix

Gareth Stevens
PUBLISHING

Please visit our website, www.garethstevens.com. For a free color catalog of all our high-quality books, call toll free 1-800-542-2595 or fax 1-877-542-2596.

Cataloging-in-Publication Data

Bix, Jasper.
Dressing for the cold / by Jasper Bix
p. cm. — (Winter fun)
Includes index.
ISBN 978-1-4824-3751-5 (pbk.)
ISBN 978-1-4824-3752-2 (6-pack)
ISBN 978-1-4824-3753-9 (library binding)
1. Clothing and dress — Cold weather conditions — Juvenile literature. I. Bix, Jasper. II. Title.
GT529.2 B59 2016
391—d23

First Edition

Published in 2016 by
Gareth Stevens Publishing
111 East 14th Street, Suite 349
New York, NY 10003

Editor: Ryan Nagelhout
Designer: Sarah Liddell

Photo credits: Cover, pp. 1, 7, 9, 11, 17, 19, 23, 24 (jacket and scarf) Digital Vision/Thinkstock.com; p. 5 al_grishin/Shutterstock.com; p. 13 Borislav Bajkic/Shutterstock.com; p. 15 Mr. High Sky/Shutterstock.com; pp. 21, 24 (boots) Brendan Howard/Shutterstock.com.

Printed in the United States of America

CPSIA compliance information: Batch #CW16GS: For further information contact Gareth Stevens, New York, New York at 1-800-542-2595.

Contents

It is cold outside
in winter.

Dress to keep warm. Winter clothes help you have fun outside.

Wear long pants.
They keep
your legs warm.

Put on a big jacket.

Make sure
you zip it up.
It keeps heat in!

13

I always wear
my gloves.

They keep
my hands warm!

My sister likes
to wear a big scarf.
It warms her neck.

Make sure
you wear boots.
They keep your feet
dry in the snow!

Don't forget a hat!

Words to Know

boot

jacket

scarf

Index

24